First North American edition published in 2013
by Boxer Books Limited.

First published in Great Britain in 2013 by Boxer Books Limited.
www.boxerbooks.com

The illustrations were prepared using ink, watercolor, and digital.
The text is set in Adobe Garamond Pro.

ISBN 978-1-907967-38-2

1 3 5 7 9 10 8 6 4 2

Printed in China

All of our papers are sourced from managed forests and renewable resources.

Ford,
Bernette
c.3

LITTLE RED RIDING HOOD

RETOLD BY BERNETTE FORD

ILLUSTRATED BY TOM KNIGHT

Boxer Books

Once upon a time, a little girl lived
with her mother at the edge of the forest.
Everyone called her Little Red Riding Hood
because her grandmother had made her
a little red cape and hood and she loved it.
In fact, she never took it off.

One sunny day, Little Red Riding Hood's
mother handed her a basket full of
baked goodies.

"Take this basket to Grandma," said Mother.

"She isn't feeling well, and these treats will help
make her feel better."

"Yes, Mother, I will," said Little Red
Riding Hood.

"Now don't stop to talk to any strangers,"
said Mother.

"And don't dilly-dally along the way."

"No, Mother, I won't," said Little Red
Riding Hood, and off she went.

Now Red Riding Hood's grandmother lived all the way on the other side of the forest. It was a long walk, but there was a lot to look at along the way.

There were birds,

and bunnies,

and chipmunks.

And there were many lovely wildflowers. Little Red Riding Hood wished she could stop and smell the flowers beside the path, but she had promised her mother not to dilly-dally. So she hurried on.

Before long, who should slink out of
the woods but a big, bad, wicked old
wolf. He stopped Red Riding Hood
on the path. Since she had never seen a
wolf before, she wasn't afraid.

"Where are you going, Little Red Riding Hood? And why are you going so fast?" asked the wolf.

"I'm on my way to Grandma's house on the other side of the forest," said Red Riding Hood. (She had forgotten her promise not to talk to any strangers.)

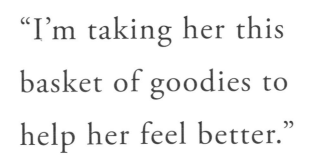

"I'm taking her this basket of goodies to help her feel better."

"But there are so many flowers here,"
said the wolf.

"I bet your Grandma would love a bouquet.
You really ought to stop and pick a pretty
bunch for her."

"That's a great idea!" exclaimed Little Red
Riding Hood.

She set down her basket and began picking wildflowers. (She had forgotten her promise not to dilly-dally along the way.)
The wolf already had a plan to have her for his lunch!

As soon as Red Riding Hood stopped by the path, the wicked old wolf ran ahead to Grandma's cottage as fast as he could. Then he knocked on her door.

"Who's there?" Grandma called from inside.

The wolf answered in a voice as sweet

as honey.

"It's Little Red Riding Hood, Grandma.

I've brought you a surprise."

When Grandma
opened the door,
the wicked old wolf
pounced!

He swallowed
her whole,
in one big gulp.

Then he put on her glasses and nightclothes and jumped into her bed. He pulled the covers up under his chin and waited for Little Red Riding Hood.

Before too long, Little Red Riding Hood
knocked on the door.

"Who's there?" called the wolf in a voice
like Grandma's.

"It's Little Red Riding Hood," she called.
"I've brought a surprise for you."

"Open the door and come in, dear," said
the wolf in his best grandmotherly voice.

Little Red Riding Hood tiptoed into the cottage. Although it was a little dim inside, she could see that her grandmother looked a bit strange.

"Why, Grandma, what big eyes you have," she said.

"The better to see
you with, my dear,"
said the wolf
in a voice like her
grandmother's.

"And Grandma, what
big EARS you have,"
said Red Riding Hood.

"The better to HEAR
you with, my dear,"
said the wolf
in Grandma's voice.

"And Grandma, what big TEETH you have,"
said Little Red Riding Hood.

"The better to EAT you with, my dear!"
snarled the wolf, and he jumped out of bed
to POUNCE on Little Red Riding Hood.

At that very
moment, a strong
young woodsman
was passing by,
and he heard the
commotion.

He broke down
the door with his ax,
just in time to
stop the wicked
old wolf and
knock him
out!

Then the woodsman zipped open his stomach,
and there was Grandma, safe and sound!
Little Red Riding Hood gave her grandmother
a big hug.

After they all had shared the baked goodies, the strong young woodsman took Little Red Riding Hood home to her mother.

Red Riding Hood promised never ever to dilly-dally or talk to strangers again!

And they all lived
happily ever after.